Copyright © 1989 Neugebauer Press, Salzburg, Austria.
Original title: "Der Fischer und seine Frau"
Published and distributed in USA by Picture Book Studio, Saxonville, MA.
Distributed in Canada by Vanwell Publishing, St. Catharines, Ont.
Published in UK by Picture Book Studio, Neugebauer Press Ltd., London.
Distributed in UK by Ragged Bears, Andover.
Distributed in Australia by Era Publications, Adelaide.
All rights reserved.
Printed in Belgium by Proost.

LIBRARY OF CONGRESS CATALOGING IN PUBLICATION DATA
The Fisherman and his wife.
Translation of: Von dem Fischer und seiner Frau.
Summary: The fisherman's greedy wife is never satisfied with the wishes
granted her by an enchanted fish.
[1. Fairy tales. 2. Folklore—Germany] I. Grimm, Jacob, 1785-1863. II. Grimm,
Wilhelm, 1786-1859. III. Marks, Alan, 1957- ill. IV. Bell, Anthea. V. Title.
PZ8.F5753        1988        398.2'2'0943        [E]        88-15165
ISBN 0-88708-072-3

Ask your bookseller for these other PICTURE BOOK STUDIO books
illustrated by Alan Marks:
NOWHERE TO BE FOUND by Alan Marks
and these others by The Brothers Grimm:
THE BRAVE LITTLE TAILOR illustrated by Eve Tharlet
THE BREMEN TOWN MUSICIANS illustrated by Josef Paleček
THE WISHING TABLE illustrated by Eve Tharlet
LITTLE RED CAP illustrated by Lisbeth Zwerger
HANSEL AND GRETEL illustrated by Lisbeth Zwerger
THE SEVEN RAVENS illustrated by Lisbeth Zwerger
SNOW WHITE AND THE SEVEN DWARVES illustrated by Chihiro Iwasaki

A Michael Neugebauer Book

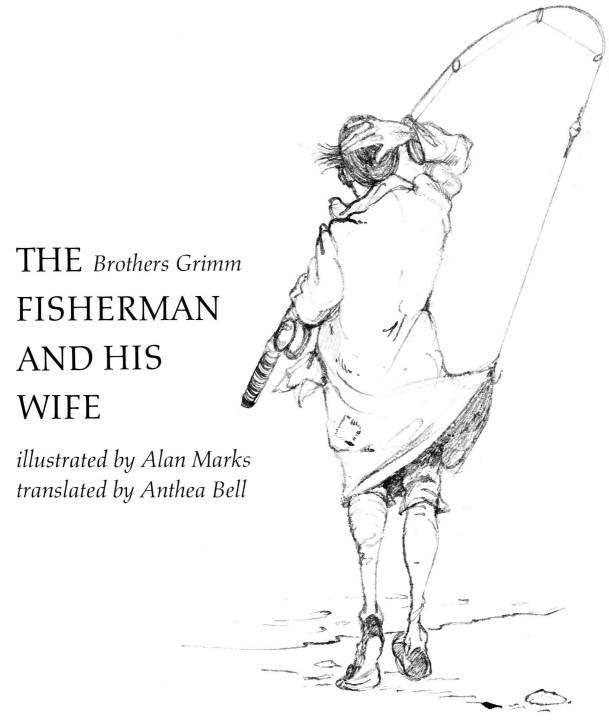

# THE *Brothers Grimm*
# FISHERMAN
# AND HIS
# WIFE

*illustrated by Alan Marks*
*translated by Anthea Bell*

*PICTURE BOOK STUDIO*

Once upon a time a fisherman and his wife lived together in a hovel by the sea. The fisherman went down to the sea every day to fish – and he fished, and he fished.

So one day he was sitting there with his rod and line, looking down into the clear water – and he sat, and he sat.

Then his line plunged deep, deep down, and when he pulled it in he found he had a great flounder on the end of it.

"Listen to me, fisherman," said the flounder, "and please let me live! I'm not a real flounder; I'm a prince under a spell. What good would it do you to kill me? You wouldn't like the taste of me – please put me back in the water and let me swim away."

"Well," said the man, "there's no need for so many words. I'd have put a talking flounder back anyway." And so saying, he put the flounder back in the clear water. The fish went right to the bottom, leaving a long trail of blood behind. Then the fisherman got up and went home to his wife in their hovel.

"Oh, husband," said the goodwife, "didn't you catch anything today?"

"No," said the fisherman. "Well, I did catch a flounder, but he said he was a prince under a spell, and I put him back again."

"Didn't you wish for anything, then?" asked his wife.

"No," said the man. "What would I wish for?"

"Well," said his wife, "it's a wretched life we lead in this stinking hovel – you might have wished for a nice little house. You just go back and call that flounder. Tell him we want to have a nice little house. I'm sure he can give us that."

"No, no," said the man. "Why would I go back there again?"

"Why?" said the woman. "You caught the flounder, and then you let him go again, so I'm sure he'll do as you ask. Off you go, then!"

The fisherman didn't really like the idea, but he didn't want to upset his wife either, so he went down to the sea again.

When he got there, the sea was all green and yellow, and the water wasn't anything like as clear as before. The fisherman went and stood on the shore, and he said:

> "Flounder, flounder in the sea,
> Swim to shore and speak to me.
> For my goodwife Isabel
> Asks for more than I dare tell."

Then the flounder came swimming up. "Well, what does she want?" he said.

"Well," said the man, "you see, I caught you, and my wife says I ought to have wished for something. She doesn't want to go on living in our hovel; she'd like to have a nice little house."

"Go home," said the flounder. "She has one now."

Then the fisherman went home, and his wife wasn't in their hovel any more. Instead, he saw a nice little house, and she was sitting on a bench outside the door. She took his hand, saying, "Come in and look at this, husband! It's much better now!"

So they went in, and the house had a little entrance hall, and a nice little living room, and a bedroom with their bed in it, a kitchen and a pantry with dishes of the very best, and tin and brass pots and pans, everything you could need. There was a little yard with chickens and ducks behind the house, and a little garden where fruit and vegetables grew.

"There!" said the goodwife. "Isn't this nice?"

"Oh, yes," said the fisherman, "and now we'll be content. We'll live very happily here."

"Well, let's think about that," said his wife, and then they ate their supper and went to bed.

So it went on for a week or so, and then the goodwife said, "Listen, husband, this house is much too small for us, and the yard and garden are very small too. The flounder might just as well have given us a bigger place. I want to live in a great big stone castle. Off you go to the flounder and tell him to give us a castle."

"Oh, wife," said the man, "this little house is quite good enough. Why would we want to live in a castle?"

"Now then," said the wife, "you just go off and tell the flounder. I'm sure he can do it."

"No, wife," said the fisherman. "The flounder's already given us this house. I don't like to go back again – he might take offense."

"Get away with you, do!" said his wife. "He can do it easily enough, and I'm sure he'd be glad to, so off you go and ask."

The man's heart was heavy, and he didn't want to go. This isn't right, he said to himself, but he went all the same.

When he came to the sea the water was all purple and dark blue and gray and thick, not green and yellow any more, but it was calm. So the fisherman stood there and said:

> "Flounder, flounder in the sea,
>   Swim to shore and speak to me.
>   For my goodwife Isabel
>   Asks for more than I dare tell."

"Well, what does she want?" said the flounder.

"Oh," said the fisherman, sadly, "she wants to live in a great big stone castle."

"Go home," said the flounder, "she's standing at the door."

The fisherman went away, thinking he would go home, but when he got there he saw a great big stone castle, with his wife standing on the steps about to go in. She took him by the hand and said, "Come along."

So he went in with her, and inside the castle there was a great hall with a marble floor, and many servants opening the great doors, and the walls were shining and covered with beautiful hangings, and there were golden tables and chairs in the rooms, and crystal chandeliers hanging from the ceilings, and carpets on all the floors. Good food and the choicest wines stood on the tables ready for them. There was a great courtyard behind the castle, with stables and cowsheds, and the grandest of carriages, and there was a beautiful great garden full of lovely flowers and handsome fruit trees, and a park half a mile long, with stags and deer and hares in it, and everything the heart could desire.

"Well," said the goodwife, "isn't this fine?"

"Oh, yes," said the fisherman, "and now we'll be content. How happy we will be, living in this wonderful castle!"

"Well, let's think about that," said the goodwife. "We'll sleep on it." And they went to bed.

Next morning the fisherman's wife was the first to wake up, when it was just day, and from her bed she saw the beautiful countryside lying there before her eyes. Her husband stretched, and she dug him in the ribs with her elbow.

"Get up, husband, and come and look out of the window," she said. "Couldn't we be kings of all this country? Go back to the flounder and tell him we want to be kings."

"Oh, wife," said the man, "why would we want to be kings? I don't want to be King."

"Well, if you don't want to be King, I do," said his wife. "Go and tell the flounder I want to be King!"

"Oh, wife," said the fisherman, "why do you want to be King? I don't like to say such a thing to the flounder!"

"Why not?" said the goodwife. "Off you go at once. I must be King!"

So off went the fisherman, very troubled in his mind because his wife wanted to be King. It's not right, he thought, it just isn't right. He didn't want to go down to the sea, but he went all the same.

And when he came to the sea it was all dark gray, and the water was rough and turbulent, and smelled foul. Then he stood on the shore and he said:

> "Flounder, flounder in the sea,
> Swim to shore and speak to me.
> For my goodwife Isabel
> Asks for more than I dare tell."

"Well, what does she want?" asked the flounder.

"Oh," said the fisherman, "she wants to be King."

"Go home," said the flounder. "She's King now."

Then the man went home, and as he came near the castle he saw that it was much larger now: it was a palace, with a great tower adorned with carving, and a sentry at the gates, and soldiers with drums and trumpets everywhere. And when he came inside, everything was made of pure marble and gold, with velvet covers that had great gold tassels on the furniture. The doors of the great hall opened; the whole court was gathered there, and his wife was sitting on a raised throne of gold and diamonds, with a great golden crown on her head, and a scepter of pure gold set with jewels in her hand, and there was a row of six ladies in waiting standing each side of the throne, each of them a head shorter than the one next to her.

The fisherman went up to her and said, "Well, wife, are you King now?" he asked.

"Yes," said the goodwife. "I'm King now."

So he stood there looking at her, and when he had been looking at her for a while he said, "Well, wife, it's a very fine thing to be King! And now we won't wish for anything more."

"Won't we, though?" said his wife, losing her temper. "This isn't good enough for me, and I'm not putting up with it any more. Go and tell the flounder that now I'm King I want to be Emperor too."

"Oh, wife," said the fisherman, "why do you want to be Emperor?"

"Husband," said she, "you just go and tell the flounder I want to be Emperor."

"Oh, wife," said the fisherman, "he can't make you Emperor; I don't want to say such a thing to the flounder. There's only one Emperor in the Empire; the flounder can't make you Emperor, and that's that."

"I'm the King," said his wife, "and you're just my husband, so will you do as I say? Off with you! If he can make me King, he can make me Emperor too, and I want to be Emperor, so off you go!"

So the fisherman had to go. But as he went down to the sea he felt very frightened. This will come to no good, he thought to himself. Emperor is just too much to ask, and the flounder will be getting tired of it all.

Then he came to the sea, and it was still all black and thick, and beginning to boil and surge so that bubbles rose to the surface, and there was a gale whipping up the water. The fisherman was afraid. But he stood on the shore and said:

> "Flounder, flounder in the sea,
> Swim to shore and speak to me.
> For my goodwife Isabel
> Asks for more than I dare tell."

"Well, what does she want now?" said the flounder.

"Oh, flounder," said he, "my wife wants to be Emperor."

"Go home," said the flounder. "She's Emperor now."

So the man went home, and when he got there he saw that the whole palace was now made of polished marble, with alabaster statues and golden ornaments. Soldiers marched up and down outside the palace, blowing trumpets and beating drums, and inside, barons and counts and dukes were going about like servants, opening doors made of pure gold for him. Once he was inside he saw his wife sitting on a throne made of a solid block of gold about two miles high. She was wearing a great golden crown six feet tall, set with diamonds and rubies, and she was holding the scepter in one hand and the imperial orb in the other. Two rows of bodyguards stood on each side of her, in order of size, from the biggest giant two miles high to the smallest dwarf no bigger than my little finger. Many dukes and princes stood before her.

Well, the man went and stood there with them, and he said, "Wife, are you Emperor now?"

"Yes," said she, "I'm Emperor now."

So he stood there looking hard at her, and after a while he said, "Well, wife, it's a very fine thing to be Emperor."

"What are you standing there for, husband?" said she. "Now that I'm Emperor I want to be Pope too. Go and tell the flounder."

"Oh, wife," said the man, "what's this you want now? You can't be Pope; there's only one Pope in all Christendom, and he can't make you Pope."

"Husband," said she, "I want to be Pope, so off you go. I want to be Pope this very day."

"No, wife, no," said the fisherman. "I don't want to tell the flounder that, it's wrong, it's too much to ask, he just can't make you Pope!"

"Nonsense, husband!" said the goodwife. "If he can make me Emperor he can make me Pope too. Be off with you! I'm Emperor and you're just my husband, so off you go!"

The fisherman was afraid, but off he went, feeling very faint, trembling and shaking, with his knees knocking together. And there was a great wind blowing over the countryside, with clouds flying, and it was all dark with night coming on. The leaves were blowing off the trees, and the water was rising and roaring and breaking on the shore, and from afar he saw ships in distress pitching and tossing in the waves. The sky had one little blue patch left in the middle, but all around the edges it was angry red, as if there were a dreadful storm coming.

The fisherman went down to the shore, feeling quite desperate, and he stood there in fear and said:

*"Flounder, flounder in the sea,*
*Swim to shore and speak to me.*
*For my goodwife Isabel*
*Asks for more than I dare tell."*

"Well, what does she want now?" asked the flounder.

"Oh," said the fisherman, "she wants to be Pope."

"Go home," said the flounder. "She's Pope now."

So he went home, and when he came there it was like a great church surrounded by palaces. He pushed his way through all the people – the place was lit up inside with thousands and thousands of lights, and his wife was dressed all in gold, sitting on an even higher throne than before, with three great golden crowns on her head, and there were churchmen of high rank all around her, and two rows of candles on each side of her, the biggest of them as thick and tall as a great high tower, and the smallest like a tiny little taper, and all the emperors and kings were on their knees in front of her kissing the toe of her slipper.

"Well, wife," said the fisherman, looking at her hard, "are you Pope now?"

"Yes," said she, "I'm Pope now."

So he stood there and looked at her, and it was like looking at the bright sun. And when he had looked at her for a while, he said, "Well, wife, what a fine thing it is to be Pope!"

She sat there stiff and straight as a post, and she didn't move a finger.

Then he said, "Be content now, wife! Be content, now you're Pope, for there's nothing more you can wish to be."

"I'll think about that," said his wife. And they went to bed, but still the goodwife wasn't content, and she couldn't sleep for greed, wondering what else she might yet be.

The fisherman slept soundly, for he had done a lot of walking that day. But his wife couldn't sleep at all; she kept tossing and turning, wondering what else she could be, but she couldn't think of anything.

Then sunrise came, and at first light of dawn she sat up in bed and looked, and when she saw the sun coming up outside the window she thought to herself, "Aha – couldn't I make the sun and the moon rise?"

"Husband," said she, digging her elbow into the fisherman's ribs, "wake up and go and tell the flounder I want to be like God."

The man was still half asleep, but he was so scared he fell out of bed. He thought he must have misheard, and rubbed his eyes. "What was that you said, wife?" he asked.

"Husband," said she, "if I can't make the sun and the moon rise, if I just have to watch them rising and I've no say in it, I can't bear it. I won't have another moment's peace if I can't make them rise myself." And she looked at him so fiercely that he shuddered. "Off you go and tell the flounder I want to be like God."

"Wife, wife!" cried the fisherman, falling on his knees before her. "The flounder can't do that. He can make you Emperor and Pope – wife, I beg you, think it over and be content with being Pope!"

Then she fell into a rage. Her hair flew about her head furiously, and she tore her nightclothes and kicked her husband, shrieking, "I can't bear it, I can't bear it – be off with you!" So he flung his breeches on and ran off like a madman.

Outside, there was such a storm he could hardly keep on his feet. The houses and the trees were shaking, the hills were trembling, rocks were rolling into the sea, the sky was black as pitch, with thunder and lightning, and the waves of the sea were black and tall as church towers or mountains, capped with crests of white foam.

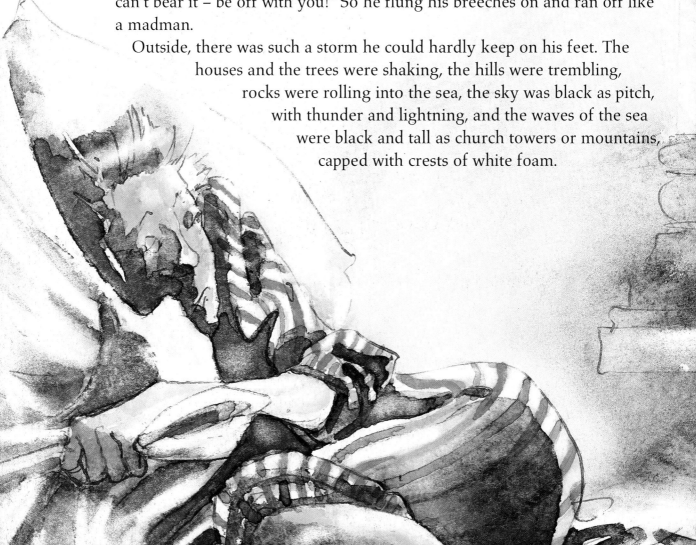

The fisherman shouted out loud, though he couldn't hear his own voice:

> *"Flounder, flounder in the sea,*
> *Swim to shore and speak to me.*
> *For my goodwife Isabel*
> *Asks for more than I dare tell."*

"Well, what does she want now?" said the flounder.
"Oh," said he, "she wants to be like God."
"Go home," said the flounder, "she's back in the old hovel."
And they're living there to this day.